Soon, Annala

STORY BY **Riki Levinson**

PICTURES BY **Julie Downing**

Orchard Books   New York

Orchard Books, 95 Madison Avenue, New York, NY 10016

Manufactured in the United States of America. Printed by Barton Press, Inc.
Bound by Horowitz/Rae. Book design by Mina Greenstein
The text of this book is set in 15 point Bembo.
The illustrations are watercolor paintings reproduced in full color.
2   4   6   8   10   9   7   5   3   1

Library of Congress Cataloging-in-Publication Data
Levinson, Riki. Soon, Annala / story by Riki Levinson ; pictures by
Julie Downing.   p.   cm. "A Richard Jackson book"—Half t.p.
Summary: While eagerly awaiting the arrival of her two younger brothers from
the old country, Anna tries to speak more English and less Yiddish.
ISBN 0-531-05494-2.   ISBN 0-531-08644-5 (lib. bdg.)
[1. Immigrants—Fiction.   2. Jews—United States—Fiction.]
I. Downing, Julie, ill.   II. Title.   PZ7.L5796So   1993   [E]—dc20   92-44588

To my mother and father
who came to America
when they were very young

—R.L.

To Fraser and Alane

—J.D.

Mama and Papa, Sister and Brother and I lived at the top of a very tall house. But my little brothers weren't with us. They were still in Kolbuszowa, with Aunt Marya.

I missed my little brothers so much, especially in the morning. Sammy and Elly used to climb into my bed and wake me up. It was almost a year since they had done that.

So every night, when Mama finished sewing and cleared off the kitchen table, I asked her, "*When* will they come?"

And every time, Mama hugged me and said, "Soon, darling. Soon."

At home, Mama and Papa spoke Yiddish. But when I talked to Sister and said *"Shvester,"* she always stopped me.

"Speak English," she said. "Say 'Sister.'"

When I first went to school, I didn't understand what the teacher was saying.

"Good morning, children," she would say.

I learned what that means. *Gut morgn, kinder.*

And when my teacher asked me to come to the front of the room, she would say, "Come here, Anna Sarah."

That means, *Kum aher, Chaya Saura.*

Big brother went to my school too. But Sister stayed home to help Mama sew. They worked every day except the Sabbath.

Sometimes Mama let me help.

After they finished all the little stitches, I pulled out the long white ones. I put them in my thread box. And when I had enough, I made a white ball and hung it at the end of my bed.

I had so many balls now. Forty-eight. They looked so pretty. And when I shook the bed, they bounced! I couldn't wait for Sammy and Elly to see them.

So again, after Mama and Sister finished their work, I asked, "*When* will they come, Mama? It's such a long time."

And Mama hugged me and said, "Very soon, Annala. Help me set the table?"

"But Mama . . . ," I said.

She pulled a paper from her pocket. "Look, children," she said.

"Oh, Mama," I gasped.

"A letter!" Sister cried.

"Of course," said Brother, like he knew about it all the time.

"I want Papa to read it to us when he comes home from work," Mama said.

I waited and waited for Papa.

When I heard him coming, I ran into the hall and called down, *"Hurry, Papa. A letter!"*

Papa laughed and ran up the last flight of stairs.

I pulled him into the kitchen. "Read it now?" I asked.

Quickly, he picked up the letter. "What have we here?" he teased.

And Papa read the letter to us.

2 August 1911
Kolbuszowa

Dearest family,

At long last, we are coming. We are so grateful for the money you sent. We have enough now for the voyage.

Our boat, the S.S. *Patricia*, should arrive in New York in a month.

Can't wait till you see our baby. The boys adore her. They send their love.

With G-d's help, we will see you soon.

Love,
Marya

Mama was crying quietly. It was such a long time since our family had been together.

But soon, very soon, we would be. I would show my little brothers our tall house, and my thread balls, and my school, and everything new in America.

Papa went to the shipping office every day to check when the boat would come.

One night, he brought a newspaper home. Papa spread it on the table and read to us. " 'Arrivals. Bremerhaven to New York. S.S. *Patricia*. September first, six A.M.' "

"Brother," I yelled, "get the calendar."

I drew a big circle around September first, and counted the days till they would come. Only seven more days!

Each morning, when I got up, I marked an X through the day on the calendar.

Finally, the day came. We went on a trolley to the harborside to wait.

Other families were waiting too.

We found a good place near the edge of the wharf with a clear view of the harbor.

I saw the Lady with a Crown—just like when we came to America.

A ferry was coming, closer and closer. The horns blew!

I covered my ears and screamed, *"They're coming. They're coming!"*

But my little brothers weren't on the ferry.

"Mama . . . ," I said, leaning against her.

"Maybe . . . the next one," she said very quietly.

Soon another ferry was coming. The horns blew!

"They're coming!" I yelled.

But I didn't see my little brothers.

"Papa . . . ," I said.

He picked me up and held me tight.

"I'm too big, Papa," I said.

Papa shook his head and held me tighter.

We waited a very long time for the next ferry.

As it came near, I saw . . . two little boys jumping up and down, waving. A man and a woman holding a baby were with them.

"Look! Look!" yelled Brother.

"Oh, Mama. Look at the baby," Sister said.

"Put me down, Papa. *They're here!*" I screamed.

When the ferry gate opened, I ran to meet my two little brothers.

"*CHAYA SAURA!*" they screamed.

"*SAMMY! ELLY!*" I shrieked.

A moment later, they broke away and ran to Mama and Papa.

Papa scooped up Sammy and Elly, and Mama wrapped her arms around the three of them, kissing them again and again.

Everybody hugged one another. Everyone was talking at the same time. We were all laughing, except Mama and Aunt Marya. They held each other close, swaying from side to side, crying.

The long wait was ended. Our whole family was together at last!

Papa, Brother, and Uncle carried the bundles to the trolley. Mama and Aunt Marya walked close behind, and Sister carried the baby. I walked with Sammy and Elly, holding their hands.

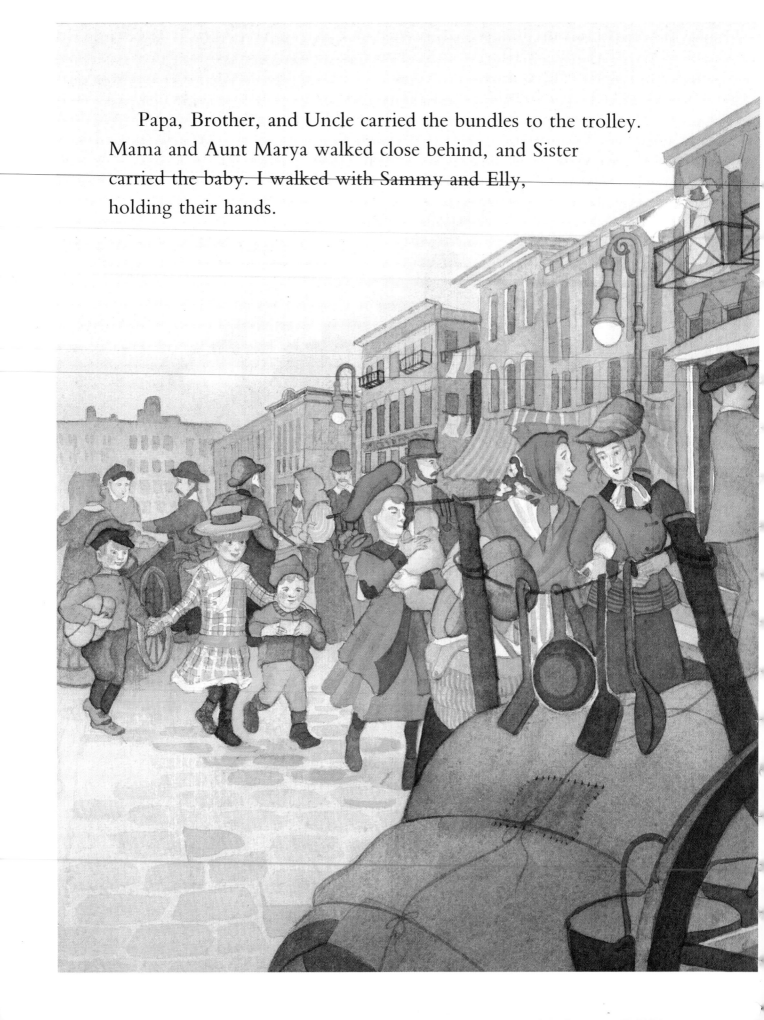

When we got home, Aunt put the baby to sleep in Mama's dresser drawer.

Everyone was talking as we sat down to eat.

Papa said a special prayer of thanks for bringing us together. Everyone was quiet, even me.

After supper, I took Sammy and Elly into my room. I shook
my bed so they could see the white balls bounce. They shook
the bed too.

We went to the window and looked at the lights shining
on the river below. And then we counted the stars as they came
out in the sky.

When I heard my little brothers say, *"Eyns, tsvey, dray,"* I
stopped them.

"In English," I said. "One, two, three."